CHAPTER ONE

"Hurry up, hurry up, we're already late, even by Unitarian standards," shouted Derek Dodd, the erstwhile companion of best friend and lover, Bettina Button, better know as Beth.

Shouting from the attached garage into the cavern of a large rambling house, Derek was reminding Beth that they were a half hour late for the important dinner at the church and she needed to introduce the speaker. THE church is the First Unitarian-Universalist of Detroit, a three building edifice built over a period of years starting in 1891. The church has seen good times and bad times and in-between times. Of late, it was having better times with some resurgence of life in the old city and in the old neighborhood, a battered and run down at the heels area just north and west of downtown.

Anyway, mumbling to herself quietly, Beth quickly got the rest of her things together in that old tote bag she liked to carry and hustled out to the car where Derek ground the gears and sped off for the fast four miles to Church via the freeway. On the way, they reviewed who the speaker was and why it was it was so important to the new life going on around and in the church.

"You know how much work it took to get the Congressman to agree to make his announcement about new money and projects? I'd better not be late or we're starting off on the wrong foot—so to speak, huh?" recited Beth.

"We'll make it, we'll make it in time for your introduction, I'm sure. These suppers never start on time and people really like to eat when it's free," Derek said firmly.

The Congressman Beth had been boning up on to introduce was none other than Congressman John Smith (yes, that's really his name—you should see when he tries to register at a hotel—nobody believes him), a well known and sometimes respected politician was going to share news about some major Federal money that could be coming the city's way. It was an important speech more for it's contents than the elocution of the speaker. And, many local people would be there. The draw was from the whole metropolitan area and would give the chance for the many ethnic and religious groups to meet and develop closer ties.

Closer ties are certainly what was called for in a city that had been known as one of the most racially divided and polarized in America. Progress had been made in bridging some of that divide in recent years with a new political climate that softened the once harsh rhetoric and made those on all sides begin to look at each other as potential allies—or at least recognize them as fellow human beings. It was important that the speech be well received and that the information in the speech give further reason for all to pull together.It was with this jumble of hopes that Beth and Derek quickly parked the car as near to the church as they could get and almost run up the steps to the Church house. They had both worked long and hard to make this night a reality—Derek as an integral part of the city planning department and Beth as a long time volunteer and activist who had worked on various projects both and outside of the church to improve race and ethnic relations and to try to bring back some economic power to a depleted city. Beth considered this work an extension of her paid job as psychotherapist at an inner city mental health clinic. And even on occasion, Beth was known to engage in amateur sleuthing, an accidental hobby brought on by the murder of one of her supposed "down and out" clients, who turned out to be the heir to a minor fortune.

Beth scurried into the main hall, smoothing her hair and putting a smile on that friendly, practical and warm face. The social hall had been added on to the sanctuary in 1917, a year after the sanctuary was built in the rose garden of the McAdow Mansion. That house had been built in 1891, when it was on the edge of the city and the streets were mud and dirt. The church house (Mansion) had a porte cochere on the side of the porch near the front door for horses to be tied up with their carriages. Detroit was not yet the Motor City!

The social hall, now called McCollester Hall after a long ago minister was not in good repair but if you didn't look closely, it was large with large windows on the alley side and a cavernous ceiling that made it seem stately.

Round tables and chairs filled the room and linen and tableware were set with a nice potted plant in the center of the table. With the lights dimmed, it looked more elegant than it was but it suited the occasion.

Diners were finishing up their dessert course having been served by young people pressed into service at the last minute and told to wear a white top and black slacks —a symbol of racial unity. Beth went over to the church's office manager, Lon Hardigan, and briefly got the run down on how things were going so far. There had been early rumors of plans to disrupt by unknown persons—perhaps by far right militia members or even far left rigid ideologues—both groups who preferred armed camps and hostility as a necessary atmosphere to maintain their power bases and feed their distrustful egos.

"Is everything okay Lon? I'm sorry we're late and I can't even blame it on Derek this time. I was running late from the job." babbled Beth.

"Everything"s going as well as can be expected. Some minor snafus but nothing to write home about." retorted Len.

"It's just about time for our introduction and then we can finally find out what money is coming and how we can make it happen."

Lon walked up to the dais and introduced Beth to Congressman Smith. They exchanged a few pleasantries while Beth checked her facts with the Congressman so she could introduce him with total accuracy. Congressman Smith's dinner plate was only half touched by him and his dessert plate was still sitting quietly in place in front of him.

He loved desserts and decided to have a few bites to energize his speech. The hall was very crowded with gobs of people and the anticipation was mounting about what plans and what MONEY might be coming Detroit's way.

Beth hushed the crowd easily and gave a short factual account of the politician's rise to office, emphasizing the more liberal policies and bills that he had supported throughout his long and usually illustrious career. She then turned to the Congressman's to stand and accept the applause that started, which he began doing, first with a smile, then with a frown then with a very puzzled look, just before he grabbed his throat, coughed with an awful sound and fell head first into his mashed potatoes.

Needless to say, there was stunned silence in the hall, like the seconds a long shot basketball throw heads toward the basket. Then the screaming and shouting began as pandemonium descended on the dinner.

"Oh, no," came from Beth's mouth and then she sat down hard with a thud. "Someonecall an ambulance and hurry." shouted Beth amid the uproar.

Despite many people rushing for the nearest exits, a young man came forward from the crowd and announced he was a doctor, newly minted.

"Can I help?" he said.

"Please, please do." begged Beth. "We need all the help we can get at this point."

The doctor, Ali Hassan, quickly took the Congressman's pulse, then said, "It's not looking good. This man appears to be dead."

"Don't say anything yet" pleaded Beth, "until things have calmed down and he can go out by ambulance in a dignified way."

"But my dear," replied Dr. Hassan, "I need to do CPR until the ambulance gets here."

"You're right, of course! What was I thinking?" Beth replied softly. "Then you'd better get to it."

Dr. Hassan immediately got help to lay the Congressman's body onto the floor and began CPR, despite the mashed potatoes still clinging to his cheeks. Despite the doctor's best efforts, no changes appeared in the Congressman's condition. He did not appear to be breathing, but what was left of the crowd was kept far back to give the doctor room to work and to protect the prostrate victim's privacy, so on one really knew what was actually happening.

The EMS personnel came running into the room. "Where is this guy?" one of the young attendants shouted.

The figure of the Congressman was quickly pointed out to him. Both the young people, one male and one female, went over to the man lying still on the floor. A pulse was taken and a stethescope tried to find a heart beat--"I think there's a faint pulse, but I'm not sure. Let's get him to Detroit Receiving right away. Maybe they can bring him around." The call was made on the radio while the Congressman was put on a stretcher with an oxygen mask over his unmoving face.

Sirens screaming into the night, the ambulance was off for the 10 block run to the Emergency Room of Detroit Receiving Hospital, the large public hospital that is a teaching arm of Wayne State University. The best care would be made available to Congressman Smith.

Once there the Congressman still on his stretcher, was whisked past all the other the others standing inside the entry way—the hospital guards, the Detroit Police contingent, the staff behind the Plexiglas window and urban poor, victims and relatives waiting to be seen for less critical conditions—on into the first available emergency medical area where doctors, nurses and ER staff came flocking to the side of the stretcher and began their usual ministrations—hooking the Congressman up to a heart machine, breathing machine, IV saline solutions going into the veins and doctors with stethoscopes, lights and concerned eyes probing the patient to determine his status.

The sterile and plain area was surrounded by hanging curtains which kept the merely curious at bay.

"His pulse is really weak." offered Dr. Nelson, one of the most experienced ER doctors at the hospital. "His blood pressure is falling. What happened?" Why is this man near death?"

"I haven't the foggiest. All we were told was he was about to give a speech and was in apparent good health, then he keeled over." replied an attending RN. "Something about choking and grabbing his throat before he toppled over," she added.

His breathing is slowing down too," noted Dr. Nelson. Let's try an emergency trachiostomy, "something is blocking his airways."

That said, the team went to work to cut a hole in the limp Congressman's throat and insert a breathing tube, but before it was in place, the heart machine flat lined and everyone heard the ominous sound. Paddles in place, electroshock was tried, but with no change. After several futile attempts, Dr. Nelson said, "Let's call it."

"7:26 PM" replied one of the nurses.

"Let's get permission for an autopsy to determine the cause of death, because this just doesn't make sense," Dr. Nelson quietly stated.

CHAPTER TWO

"Anaphylactic shock, that's what killed him, and it looks like it was murder," suggested Lt. McCleary of the Detroit Police Department, "not an accident."

"Why are you sure it was murder?" asked Beth, who was being briefed, along with Rev. Stewart, in order to obtain all the details of what had happened that fateful evening.

The DPD was leaving no stone unturned to try to find those responsible as it was looking like a blight on the city—again.

"Because no one else had peanut oil in their dessert, only the Congressman. And because the Congressman was VERY allergic to peanuts as he had had previous episodes where he almost died from ingesting just a little bit of peanuts. It wasn't widely known that he had this allergy, but somebody knew and made use of it."

"Anaphylectic shock is cumulative, unlike most other allergies. Every time you ingest some of the allergic substance, you have a stronger and stronger reaction, until your system can't take it anymore and shuts down. It works on the respiratory system almost instantly and causes the bronchial tubes et al to constrict to the point that the person can't breathe. His heart shuts down when the breathing stops."

"So I repeat," queried the Lt., "who could have known about his allergy and who could have wanted him dead?"

Beth and Derek looked at each other and shrugged their shoulders helplessly.

"I haven't the foggiest notion," replied Beth and Derek shook his head in agreement.

CHAPTER THREE

"So now what do we do?" asked Derek.

Beth replied that she didn't know but that they needed to go home and get some rest. "Maybe we'll think clearer in the morning."

Well, it's now morning and Beth and Derek had trouble sleeping during the night, struggling with the notion that someone had murdered a man in their church hall. A church that stood for peace, non-violence and love.

"How could this have happened?" said Beth. Derek just shook his head in continued disbelief.

Beth said, "I'm going to go down to the church this morning and nose around,see if anything stands out but the police will probably already have gone over everything, I would imagine." I don't have any appointments this morning so I can take the time to do this."

"Okay," said Derek, but be careful will you?"

"Of course", replied Beth.

As Beth drove over to church, she kept thinking who would want the Congressman dead and why? He had made some enemies with his liberal policies and some thought he spent too much money on poor people. Those same people also thought that if you were poor, it was your fault and you should just go get a job, not recognizing the lingering effects of poverty, racism and generational history. The Declaration of Independence said we were all born equal, but Beth knew that was not so. Many people were born with advantages of money, education and good nutrition. Others were born into families that had little money, little formal education, a long standing history of poor health and poor nutrition.

"But you can't automatically assume it's some right wing fanatic that killed him, can you?" she thought. Although historically in the United States, most public figure assassinations have been of more liberal thinkers by the more conservative. Think of Abraham Lincoln, John F. Kennedy, Rev. Martin Luther King, Jr. and Robert F. Kennedy. Maybe the right wing are better shots since they are often enamored of guns and weapons. Some right wing politicians have been shot but didn't die, ie: George Wallace and Ronald Reagan.

Beth was soon at the church complex, parked in the church parking lot and went into the building with the key she had been given as she frequently helped out with events there and needed easy access. There were a few cars in the lot but otherwise, everything seemed quiet and normal, with Wayne State students walking by in small groups or alone, on their way to classes. It was hard to believe that a man had died less than 24 hours ago in this same building.

There was no crime scene tape outside the building or even inside as the police had apparently been there all night canvassing the scene and area for any clues as to what happened.

Beth walked back to the kitchen where things were in disarray—items were sitting helter-skelter on the floor, on the counters and there was dust and what appeared to be finger print powder everywhere.

"What am I looking for?" thought Beth.

She wandered around the kitchen and noted the mess but realized she had no way to clean it up and anyway, someone at the church who was in charge of cleaning would be the appropriate person to do this. She didn't see any glaring signs of peanut oil or peanut products at first. But whoever had put this in the Congressman's food wouldn't have left it around for others to find, would they?

Then she saw it! Hidden beyond the paper towel roll at the back of a counter was a small jar of peanut butter!

"How did this get missed?" thought Beth. She knew she shouldn't touch it herself so took a cloth towel and picked it up and looked at the peanut butter jar.

Just then a person entered the kitchen which startled Beth. It was one of the young men who lived on the third floor of the church house who did janitorial work for a free room. They had to buy their own food and cook it but they also kept the church complex mostly clean.

"Who are you?" asked the young man.

"I'm Bettina Button, better known as Beth", Beth replied. "And who are you?, she said.

"I'm Timothy Trotter", he answered.

Beth explained that she was a long time member of the church and was at the dinner the night before when Congressman Smith had died and she just wanted to help find out what had happened.

"And did you?" asked Timothy.

"Well, I just found the jar of peanut butter and wondered how it got there, said Beth.

"Oh, that's nothing. That's mine." replied Timothy. "I usually eat peanut butter on toast for breakfast most mornings."

"Well, don't you think the police should know about this?" countered Beth.

"I don't see why" said Timothy. "I just brought it down from upstairs."

"Oh, okay" said Beth, but still wondering if this was relevant to the police inquiry.

Since she didn't have any authority in the investigation, she reluctantly gave Timothy the jar of peanut butter and went back to her car. But she then quickly called the Detroit Police Department and asked to speak to the person in charge of the investigation. She was connected to Sgt. Jones who brusquely asked what she wanted.

CHAPTER FOUR

"My name is Bettina Buttons and I was just at the Unitarian Church in the kitchen.I had been at the dinner the night before when Congressman Smith died and thought I'd check out the church kitchen this morning." offered Beth.

"Well, you should leave this to the police, young lady," said Sgt. Jones.

"I agree the police are in charge but I wanted you to know that I just found a jar of peanut butter in the kitchen that supposedly belongs to a man named Timothy who lives upstairs. I though you should know this." Beth replied.

"Well, that went well---not" thought Beth. As she hung up the phone, she decided that she would have to do some more investigating on her own since the police didn't seem interested in what she found.

"Who is that guy, Timothy and where did he come from?" Beth knew she would have to do some detecting and see where it led. In the past, she had helped uncover a killer that was threatening women in her neighborhood, mostly by accident, when the killer started stalking Beth and she was omniscient enough to figure this out before he could kill her too. It was a scary time but she survived and thought that it had made her a stronger person.

"What is the first thing I need to do?" thought Beth. She decided to contact the church minister, the Rev. Andrea Stewart, who had recently become First UU's settled minister. Rev. Stewart was the first African-

American minister that the church had called. She had come from a small UU church in Illinois and was well recommended. This was her second year at the Detroit church.

Beth called Rev. Stewart who answered immediately and agreed to meet Beth for coffee at a nearby restaurant on the Wayne State campus.

Beth could easily walk to the restaurant which she did, went in, got her coffee and settled at a table near the door. About 20 minutes later, Rev. Stewart walked in and spied Beth easily. The Rev. got her coffee and went to Beth's table and said, "What'sthis all about, Beth?"

"Well, you know about the congressman who died last night after eating some food at our dinner, right?"

"Yes, the police contacted me as a formality. I wasn't able to be at the dinner, I was visiting a critically ill member in the hospital and thought I needed to spend most of the evening with her. But it's a tragedy what happened, isn't it?" said the Rev.

"It was more than a tragedy, I think it was murder." replied Beth.

"Murder? Oh my heavens!, that can't be.?" puzzled the minister.

"Well he was the only one who was allergic to peanuts and died from anaphalayctic shock His food was the only one that had some form of peanuts in it according to the police, so it looks like an intentional death to me," answered Beth.

"Yes, it does look like that, doesn't it?" replied Rev. Stewart.

"But Beth, call me Andrea. What can I do to help?"

"For starters, tell me about a guy named Timothy who

he recently came here from New York. I think it was Alex May who recommended him. He gave some references and we checked them out. He seemed to be okay. Why? Is there a problem?" asked Marilyn.

Beth replied, "I don't know, but he was acting kind of squirrely when I encountered him in the kitchen this morning. He had some peanut butter out and seemed offended that I was asking him about it. You know the Congressman died from eating some kind of peanut product, don't you?"

"Actually, I didn't know that." said Marilyn. "Wow! That's weird, isn't it?"

"And when I tried to talk to the police about this, they blew me off." was Beth's reply. "I'm just trying to find out what happened!"

Marilyn said "I'll help any way I can. Let me call Dan East and see what he knows."

Dan East was the Vice President of the Church Board and did some of everything around the church. He was always at the church helping fix things and supervising others who were helping.

"Ok, let me know what he says, if anything." countered Beth.

CHAPTER SIX

Beth and Derek had a simple meal planned for dinner so Beth went about fixing it. They lived in an older house near the downtown area but liked the neighborhood. There was a neighborhood association and most of the residents worked in the city. They had bought their house when home prices in the city were really low so they felt they got a bargain, but had to keep putting some money into it to keep everything working and to modernize as much as possible.
The kitchen was a large room at the back of the house and they had been able to buy some newer appliances which made cooking and maintenance easier. They both tried to stay away from red meat because of the way the animals were treated but sometimes had pepperoni on pizza, which they couldn't resist.

With dinner out of the way, Beth and Derek looked at each other with quizzical gazes.

"Let's sit down and talk." said Derek.

Beth replied, "Okay."

She then brought him up to speed on what she had done during the day and what she had learned so far, ie: the police were not interested in her information that she had found a new member of the church house staff with peanut butter and that he hadn't been very forthcoming. Also that she had talked to Rev. Stewart and the Board President but otherwise, no one knew anything for sure.

"Beth, you need to be careful. Remember what almost happened the last time you tried to help."

"I know." said Beth, "but I can't just sit here and do nothing. I'll be extra careful. I'm just going to chat with

City with an address in Harlem. That was interesting as Timothy looked to be of European descent. But it listed the age of 23 and that seemed about right to Beth's eye.

Beth had a long time friend who had moved to NYC two years ago so she decided to give her friend a call.

"Hi, Beth," said Fatima, a young woman whom Beth had met in graduate school and with whom she had formed an instant bond as both Beth and Fatima were very interested in social justice issues. "What's going on?"

"Well, I'm wanting to pick your brain about something" So Beth proceeded to tell Fatima all about the death of Congressman Smith and how she, Beth, was trying to find out more about who might have wanted to kill the Congressman.

Beth and Fatima also talked about what each was doing. Fatima said that New York City was way different from Detroit and how it took some getting used to—all the hustle and bustle all the time and the noise level! But Fatima agreed to check out the address for Timothy Trotter and get back to Beth as soon as possible.

CHAPTER EIGHT

Well, let's see what Fatima can find out, thought Beth. In the meantime, she and Derek had supper and spent a relaxing evening at home watching some mindless TV shows.

Both Derek and Beth were busy for the next few days and no other news was reported about the death/murder of Congressman Smith. The Detroit Police Sergeant never called Beth back.

But Beth had begun to learn more about the announcement that the Congressman was going to make at the dinner. One of his staff, with whom she was fairly good friends, let her know that the announcement was that the city of Detroit was going to be awarded an large sum of money (about $250 million) to deal with blight, decrease crime and help home owners take care of their property so that more houses didn't fall into disrepair. It was unclear if this money would still be appropriated but time would tell. Certainly Detroit needed all the help it could get in tearing down the thousands of abandoned homes that were scattered all over the city, but particularly on the east side. As the population left Detroit to go to the suburbs (mostly the white population) and then with the ongoing foreclosure crisis, a city of primarily single family home owners spread over 139 square miles had taken a huge hit which effected both individuals and the entire city, financially and emotionally.

Beth vowed to do what she could to see that the large appropriation would still happen.

"But what now?", thought Beth. "I know! Derek

works in the City Planning Office. Maybe he would know who to ask."

Beth called Derek and told him of her dilemma. He agreed to check with his co-workers and see if anyone knew someone who could tell them about the possible appropriation. Derek said he would let Beth know that evening when he got home from work.

Beth also went to work and took on several new clients. Many of her old clients had been stablized with the combination of medications and individual therapy, so some of them needed to come in only every 3 months to for a psychiatric review by the doctor. It felt good to know that some people had improved their lives and were doing so much better. Some were even able to take on part time jobs to supplement their meager incomes.

Now and then, Beth got a new client who was hard to work with and sometimes hard to even like. Such a client now sat in front of Beth as she took down his social history and tried to determine what his problems were and how best to treat him.

His name was Bill Duncan (I always change the names of clients and never give out real names in keeping with confidentiality agreements). Bill was a 25 year old European American who was born and raised in the South—South Carolina to be exact.

He presented as angry at the world and at Black people in particular. He reported having been raised by parents who was very poor and were also alcoholic. He talked of being beaten with sticks and 2x4's, often for little reason. Both his parents were now dead but he carried his hatred for them in his heart and mind.

He also felt that Black people had been given many things that he never got, ie: Medicaid and food stamps. He had moved North at the age of 18 because he thought he could get a good factory job but by the time he arrived, many plants were not hiring as the country was in a small recession. He did get a low paying job as a dishwasher at a downtown restaurant but he often argued with the other staff and was finally told that he had to see a counselor to get help or he would be fired. So, needless to say, he reluctantly came into the clinic seeking "help."

"I don't need no help, lady." Bill asserted. "There's nothing wrong with me. The world is a terrible place and people don't like it when I tell the truth."

He had applied for Medicaid and food stamps but earned just a little too much to be eligible, hence his feeling that he was being shortchanged while "Blacks" got all the breaks. He had no other family and no real friends.

Beth saw an angry, depressed man in front of her and wondered how to help him. She did listen carefully to what he said and gave him positive affirmation of what his feelings were but did not acknowledge that his reasons for negative feelings were reality based. She did try to give him some compliments on positive things that she heard—told him it was brave of him to leave his home state and come to a place where he knew no one and start a new life.

She encouraged him to think about anything or anyone that made him feel good without increasing his feelings of anger, but he said that he basically didn't trust people and the only positive feeling he had was when he had a gun in his hand--that made him feel powerful and unstoppable.

"Wow" thought Beth. "This guy is scary!"

"Okay, now what do I do?" ran through Beth's mind. But her usual optimism told her that she would continue to work with him and try her best to help him get to a better place in his head and heart.

Beth continued seeing her clients for the rest of the day and since it was such a nice sunny day, as she walked home, she noted the trees full of fall color, the birds singing, and some squirrels trying to hide nuts for the winter. Beth felt more peaceful than she had in a while. As she got home, her phone rang, so she answered it.

It was her friend, Fatima, in New York City. "I went to the address listed for Timothy Trotter and it was some kind of politically based storefront that appeared to be quite right of center." said Fatima. "The people going in there were all wearing beards, had long hair and were men. They looked to be in their 20's and 30's," furthered Fatima. "The name on the storefront read Make America Free. I looked up what that meant and it appears to be a political action group that wants to do away with most laws and let people do whatever they want to, like smoke Marijuana in public, make all drugs legal and lower taxes way down so that the federal government has little power and very little money. At least that's what it said on their website. What do you think, Beth?"

"Sounds very radical", said Beth. "What I wonder is why this guy came to Detroit just a few weeks ago and is staying at a UU church house? Could he have had an ulterior motive in coming here?--like killing a Congressman who didn't agree with his beliefs? Makes you wonder?"

"Well, be careful, Beth." offered Fatima. "He doesn't sound like he's wrapped too tight!"

"Oh, I'll be careful" countered Beth. I'll do some checking here but keep a low profile."

CHAPTER NINE

So when Derek got home from work, Beth told him what Fatima had found out and asked Derek what he had learned? Derek then proceeded to tell Beth what he had learned at City Hall where he worked as an urban planner. It turns out that Congressman Smith had planned to announce that a large sum of money would be coming to Detroit and was to be funneled through the city government to build on what services already existed, which Derek thought would be a good thing.

However, Congressman Smith was known as a womanizer and it seems that a big scandal was about to be unleashed, ie: his wife was going to file for divorce and claim that his top assistant was having an affair with the Congressman. How that would have effected everything was still unclear.

"Wow" said Beth, "that could have been messy and maybe still will be. What do you think Derek?"

"Well, I think the scandal may still come out but it may wait awhile until after his funeral services and may only be a footnote at this point. However, it does add to the mix as to who or whom might want him dead."

"This makes everything more complicated rather than less." mused Beth. "How can we find out more about this Tim Trotter guy just to see if he came here to kill the Congressman?"

Derek replied that he knew a couple of the guys who lived upstairs in the church house so he would try to talk with them and see if he could find out more about Tim Trotter.

"Sounds like a plan" said Beth.

The next morning both Derek and Beth left for work, not forgetting to feed and pay some attention to their cat named "Charity" who Beth had gotten from the Humane Society several years ago. Charity was a mellow cat and liked to sleep a lot so that worked out well as she had to stay at home alone most days.

Beth had a long list of clients to see that day starting with a woman named Melanie who was struggling with addiction problems and an abusive husband at home. Beth had been seeing Melanie for about two years now and had made some progress very incrementally. Melanie was now on Suboxone prescribed by the clinic psychiatrist so she wouldn't use Heroin or pills and she had begun to stand up to her husband in small ways, but not so obviously that would incur his wrath.

Beth was encouraging Melanie to improve her self esteem by using positive affirmations on a daily basis and by helping Melanie to see that her abusive parents had set her up to marry an abusive partner. Melanie was even considering leaving her husband if he remained abusive but that had to be planned very carefully to lessen the danger to Melanie as the moment a person leaves an abusive partner is when that partner will lash out to remain in control.

After Melanie left, Beth had a few moments to chat with her co-workers before her next client. Most of the other therapists were female and were a mix of Euro-American, African-American and Hispanic American as the Detroit area was a mix of many groups and cultures with the majority of Detroiters being African-American.

Several of the other therapists were close to Beth in

age while most others were older females. Beth enjoyed sharing stories of clients and discussing treatment techniques and resources. There was always something more to learn. One of therapists with whom Beth had become fairly close friends was named Karen Gardner and they sometimes went out to lunch together to nearby restaurants but not today.

Karen and Beth were having a snack in the break room and Beth was telling Karen about the death of Congressman Smith. Karen had read about it in the papers but not much information had been given about the cause and circumstances of his death. Karen was surprised to realize that the death was likely murder. Beth shared the outline of what she had found out so far but in talking it out, realized that she really didn't have much actual information, only suspicions and suppositions.

As Karen and Beth talked, Beth realized that she was going nowhere fast. What to do next?

That question would have to wait for awhile as Beth then saw her next client, an older man named Brian Olesky who had started seeing Beth several months ago for feeling depressed related to chronic back pain and limited mobility. In addition, he was having trouble getting appropriate pain medication due to the current thrust to limit addicting pain meds because of the opiod crisis.

Brian was friendly and seemed to enjoy having someone to talk with and vent to. His marriage was not good and he and his wife had little contact with each other even though they lived in the same house. He felt that his wife took every opportunity to belittle him and he, in turn, had little love left for his wife. He claimed that she had done some things behind his back, such as signing the house away to another relative,which he found out by accident. His income was very limited as he was on Social Security Disability with little to no pension.

So the usual messy mix of people's problems. "Why do I enjoy doing this work?" thought Beth. "I guess I really like seeing people feel better and learn how to cope with all that life has thrown at them" answered Beth to herself. "Somehow I'm righting some wrongs and that feels good."

So after another busy day, she wended her way home and fed Charity and started getting supper ready for her and Derek. She decided on fixing a large salad with many veggies and some left over white meat chicken to use as protein. This was easy and fast. The kitchen in her old house was large but not very modern. However, it would do for now. She and Derek had thought about getting married and then buying a house in a little bit nicer neighborhood but they weren't quite ready to make that commitment.

Derek came through the door just as she finished preparing dinner so both sat down to eat and review their day.

Beth said a little about her clients without giving any names, of course, but Derek said he had learned some things. He had stopped off at the church house after leaving work a little early and was able to talk with several of the church house residents. One in particular named Rod said he was concerned about their new roommate, Tim Trotter, so was keeping an eye on him.

Something didn't just sit right with Rod. He said that Tim did the work required but said very little and wasn't really interacting with the rest of them. He didn't know about Tim's political views as Tim made no comments about political issues but when Derek told Rod about the group in New York where Tim had been living, Rod was surprised. He said that that group was actually sort of a "right wing" group with ideas of condoning violence to get their way. Rod wondered why Tim would want to live with a group that was more left of center and thus quite contrary to his own supposed views? Rod agreed to continue observing Tim and would let Derek know of anything of consequence that came up.

CHAPTER TEN

It was at about that point that both Derek and Beth noticed that their cat, Charity, was crying and throwing up blood.

"What going on with Charity?" said both Beth and Derek at the same time.

All thoughts of detection went out the window as Beth got the cat carrier and Derek got the car out to take Charity to an emergency vet that was some miles away. Neither had noticed anything wrong with the cat before that evening which is what they told the vet tech when they arrived at the emergency clinic.

"This may take a few minutes." said the tech. We'll check her out and ask you to wait in the waiting room.

After a good half hour, the tech came out and took them back to a room where the vet was petting Charity who looked unhappy but who was no longer crying or throwing up.

"What happened to our cat?" anguished Beth.

"Well, it looks like she ingested something that poisonous to her. I think it may have been some kind of chemical that's found in cleaning supplies, but I'm not sure." replied Dr. Watson.

"Oh no" replied Beth. "We thought we were so careful and kept all cleaning stuff behind cabinet doors."

"Cats are very clever at getting in where they shouldn't and sometimes it causes them problems, so go home and check out where you have your cleaning supplies and see if anything looks tampered with." cautioned Dr. Watson. "I've given her something as an antidote and something to calm her stomach down, so she should be all right, but keep an eye on her for the next several days and bring her back if she shows symptoms again."

"Thank you Doctor." Derek was shaken but glad that it looked like Charity would survive.

When they got home, they immediately went to the area below the kitchen sink where they kept most of their cleaning supplies and sure enough, there was a plastic bottle of Drano that had a small hole in it toward the top of the bottle which was easily noticeable. They quickly threw out the bottle after wrapping it in a plastic bag and putting it in the trash can with the top on tight so Charity couldn't easily get to it. Maybe it tasted sweet or something thought Beth. Anyway, Charity went and laid down in her cat bed near the stove and went to sleep after a traumatic evening.

Beth and Derek were also exhausted and realizing they would have to replan their bills as the vet bill had been a large one but it was all in a good cause.

"Another day, another dollar and a half," quoted Derek as he and Beth left for work

at the same time the next morning.

"What will the day bring?" said Beth and hoped for some movement in the effort to find out how killed the Congressman.

CHAPTER ELEVEN

While Beth and Derek went about their day, Tim Trotter was scowling and looking angry. He thought he heard people talking about him and not in a good way. Why did people always suspect him of doing something bad. He was a God fearing good guy, but nobody every gave him a chance to prove it. He was tired of being put down and had decided some time ago to get back at those who constantly wronged him.

"What could I do to make people realize that I'm somebody, not a nobody?" thought Tim. He did the work that was required of him to keep the church and grounds presentable but did a half-assed job, not even realizing this. He had had a very troubled childhood with an alcoholic mother who frequently berated him and told him he wouldn't amount to anything, but who also had never taught him how to clean anything properly. His father was mostly absent and also very negative toward Tim. He left home at age 16 after dropping out of high school with lackluster grades. He had moved to New York City from a small town in upstate New York thinking that he would find a place for himself in the "Big Apple." But that was not to be. He got jobs washing dishes and doing janitorial work but since he didn't do his jobs well, he was often let go, not understanding what he was doing wrong.

He had ended up at the Make America Free storefront office because they let him stay there and keep an eye on the place to act as a deterrent to anyone coming in and trying to cause trouble. Tim had felt more accepted there than anywhere else he had lived but didn't understand what the philosophy of the group, choosing to not listen very well when members of the group came in and started shouting about how bad the federal government was and why it needed to change and stop telling people what to do.

By accident, he had learned about a church in Detroit that let people live there in return to doing some janitorial work.

"I can do that," thought Tim so managed to get someone to give him a work reference (possibly to get rid of him) and that resulted in his taking a bus to Detroit and showing up at the First Unitarian-Universalist church house with a letter of introduction. He had few possessions, all of which fitted into a single suitcase.

"Things will be different here." said Tim to himself as he settled into the job.

CHAPTER TWELVE

In the meantime, as they say in novels, Beth had started her day as a therapist and was not looking forward to seeing her next client, Julia Bunting. Julia was someone Beth had been seeing for several years with little progress to show for it. Julia, aged 64, enjoyed coming to see Beth but presented and acted like a child, bemoaning why no one cared about her and in general seeing herself as a victim. She came from a large white working class family whose father was a working alcoholic and whose mother was busy with too many children to give any one of them enough attention.

Julia had little formal education and had worked primarily as a waitress. She did marry one time to a severely overweight man when she was living in Florida, but they divorced after a few years with no children. She had moved back to Michigan and did some office work, finally developing some physical problems that allowed her to receive Social Security Disability payments.

When Beth first met her, Julia was staying in an apartment and had let an alcoholic brother move in with her while he healed from a broken leg. Needless to say, they didn't get along very well but he had a car and did drive, so he brought her to appointments almost weekly. She wondered why she had few friends and her relationships with her siblings and their children was fraught with drama much of the time. Julia always thought it was someone else's fault if there was a problem and saw herself as the innocent.

In addition, Julia was seeing the clinic psychiatrist, Dr.

Sterling, who was treating her for Major Depression, but the medication he prescribed didn't seem to help much, or at least, Julia claimed it didn't. Dr. Sterling kept changing the medications trying to find something that might lighten her mood but so far, no change. And, of course, Julia made negative comments to Beth about the doctor.

Mostly all Beth could do was let Julia ventilate and offer some positive feedback if and when Julia actually made a positive statement. Julia seemed to see Beth as her "friend" which Beth kept trying to explain to Julia wasn't the nature of the therapeutic relationship.

CHAPTER THIRTEEN

Now was the day for Congressman's Smith's funeral, an event that took place at Hartford Memorial Baptist Church, a church where the Congressman had been a member for many years and which was a large old church on the city's west side.

However, it could barely contain the crowd who came out to pay their last respects to the Congressman. The Vice-President of the United States was there to speak, along with the city's Mayor and other dignitaries. It was being televised on national TV with all the hoopla that entails.

Beth and Derek felt obligated to go and the Congressman was in fact their Congress person for whom they had both voted. They got there a little early and managed to find a parking space several blocks from the church. Luckily, the weather was relatively mild so they could walk to the church and managed to squeeze in at the back of the church and actually get seats. Many who came later had to stand for the entire two hour service.

The Detroit police were there in force to prevent any problems and also to see if anyone showed up who looked suspicions as they were still trying to solve the murder case.

As the strains of Amazing Grace wafted through the sanctuary at the close of the service, Beth kept thinking "Who would want Congressman Smith dead? It didn't make any sense. "Amazing Grace, how sweet the sound, who saved a wretch like me?"
Who was the wretch that needed saving?

Beth didn't see anyone who looked particularly suspicious. Everyone just looked sad, many were crying. Congressman Smith had served his congressional district in Detroit for 40 years and as far as she knew, was considered a "good guy", one of the US representatives who provided good constituent services. He was voted back in 20 times so he must have been doing something right.

Beth and Derek left the church feeling a little down and both had to get back to their jobs. The sky was cloudy and gray in keeping with the mood. The other mourners were also walking back to their cars and the only sounds that broke the silence were the sounds of birds singing.

"How odd!" thought Derek. "But I guess birds sing no matter what."

Derek went back downtown to the City County building which was his base of operation. He was still in a somber mood. Something just didn't feel right. He went to his boss and asked to take the rest of the day off as he had lots of overtime and was granted his request.

With that done, he went back to his car and the day was starting to get cloudy. It looked like it would rain soon. He better get where he was going before he got soaked.

Derek drove to the First U-U Church and parked in the front of the church house, quickly running up the front steps and rang the bell. The church office manager pressed the buzzer and let him in. He went to the office and said Hi. to office manager, Lon Hardigan. Lon had been hired to work part time five days a week and to also provide some security at the building complex.

He had been there for five years now and seemed to be doing a good job. Lon was a tall thin man with graying hair who was minimally friendly but kept an even temperament and was very alert to what was going on around him. He didn't talk a lot and seemed able to keep a confidence when asked, so Derek got right to it and said that he was wondering about the new upstairs tenant, Tim Trotter, and wondered what Lon thought of him.

Lon paused before saying that he, too, wondered about Tim, who seemed to be a loner in many ways and seemed to have little self awareness and how he presented to others. Tim was reported to do the minimum amount of work required of him and wasn't a very thorough cleaner but the others were trying to be patient and teach him how to do a better job. But something just doesn't sit right with me about him.

"Do you think you could check out his room when he's not there just to make sure there is nothing to be afraid of with him?" suggested Derek.

"Well, technically, it's probably illegal but he is living on church grounds and his behavior is strange, so I'll think about it and get back to you." said Lon.

"That's fair enough." replied Derek.

Derek decided it would be best for him to go home briefly and check on how Charity was doing. She had been really sick, seemed better, but not fully recovered yet.

When he went into their house, there was no sign of the cat. She usually greeted either Beth or Derek with meows and wanting to be petted. So Derek went around the house looking for Charity. He finally found her lying on their bed upstairs. She was sleeping soundly but didn't seem upset. He gently petted her and she opened up her eyes and looked at him expectantly. He continued petting her and talking to her as she gradually woke up. Derek was thinking that the strong antibiotics that they had to give her to counteract the poisoning probably made her sleepy but called the vet's office just to make sure. The vet tech agreed that Charity sleeping a lot was likely the result of the strong meds. she was taking but said to bring her in again if she didn't show signs of becoming more lively as the days wore on.

"Well that's a relief." thought Derek. He continued to check on Charity who was becoming more awake and started to move around the house.

Derek sat down in the living room to pause and think about all that had happened and to try to figure out what the heck was going on. No brilliant thoughts came to him but he still focused on Tim Trotter and thought that there was a good likelihood that Tim had something to do with the Congressman's death. But how to prove it?

In the meantime, Beth had gone to work and had a full schedule of clients to see today. The first one was a person who had made good progress on lessening her anxiety and learning to live with chronic pain—Carol Gerber.

Carol had gone through a divorce and had joint custody of a daughter with her ex-husband and had remarried but several years ago but had serious problems with her back, resulting in multiple surgeries with limited range of motion and constant pain for which she did not want to take opiates as she knew how addicting they were.

So she walked with a cane and did some exercises to stay as fit as she could. Carol had worked as an accountant and was quite intelligent and organized. But she enjoyed coming to see Beth monthly for "talk therapy" and also saw the clinic psychiatrist monthly for psych meds. She was on an anti-anxiety medication and an antidepressant med which seemed to working fairly well.

Today, Carol talked about how proud she was of her daughter who was finishing high school and getting ready to go to college. Carol had been so organized that she had quietly saved $40, 000 for her daughter's education so that her daughter could go to college and not have to take out student loans. Carol had been granted Social Security disability several years ago and was considered too disabled to work for a living. Carol's daughter had good grades and was accepted at several Michigan colleges. She just had to decide where to go.

It was rewarding to see a client feel better, Beth felt a sense of accomplishment. Most of her clients seemed to improve but there were a few who didn't and asked for a different therapist.

One such person was a young man, named Brent Jackson. He had come to counseling voluntarily, seeking help with chronic depression and a life long history of being so introverted that he had few, if any, friends. Brent was a young Euro-American, aged 22, who had finished college and was working at an office job that was "okay" but he seemed to have no real sense of purpose and few interests. It turns out that Brent had been raised by a very successful father who was a medical doctor but whowas also extremely physically abusive to he and his brothers and a mother who didn't intervene and for financial reason didn't leave her husband..

Eventually it turned out that the father was a pill addict who ended up losing his practice and plunging the family into debt and dire financial straits. His father did get treatment and was doing better but the family was far from reconciled.

When Brent started therapy, he was quiet and it took much encouragement to get him to talk at all. Although he continued coming to therapy, it wasn't going well when finally Brent asked Beth's supervisor for a different therapist. She felt badly that she hadn't been able to help but suggested a male therapist and it turned out that Brent seemed to make some progress after he began seeing the new therapist.

"Well, should I or shouldn't I?" thought Lon but he had already made his mind up that he would go up on the third floor of the church house and do some exploring when he knew the residents would not be there.

So up he went with some feelings of trepidation but went anyway. He used the emergency key that was kept in the church office for the third floor. No one else seemed to be in the building but he walked quietly and after knocking and hearing no response, he unlocked the door and stepped inside.

It was primarily a large dormitory but there was also a small kitchen, a small living room that housed a television set and a communal bathroom. The dormitory took up the front half of the attic space and hadn't had any work done on it for years so it looked shabby but functional. He noticed that clothes were strewn all about which didn't surprise him since there were six men living there at the moment. And, God Forbid, while he tried not to be a sexist, it appeared that these guys weren't into housekeeping.

Lon wandered around trying to figure out who slept where and if Tim Trotter had his own area. Sure enough, over in a corner under the eaves, he found what looked like some of Tim's clothing and an unmade bed. He kept nosing around and saw that Tim had some food items stashed in a paper bag near his bed. Lon felt funny but also thought that what he was doing had to be done. "Who was this guy?"

Lon looked more closely into the bag and thought he saw a small bottle of some kind of liquid. "What is that?" and "What do I do now?"

Lon decided to call Beth who was able to talk to him when he called. After Lon explained what he had found, Beth insisted that Lon call Sgt. Jones at the Detroit Police Station and tell him he may have found.

Lon wasn't looking forward to doing that but figured he had no other choice. Amazingly enough, Sgt. Jones was actually friendly and said that the police had just gotten a search warrant to search every room in the church house as they had no other leads or clues about who had killed the Congressman. Sgt. Jones said he would be right over and told Lon not to let anyone else into the church house.

CHAPTER FOURTEEN

When Sgt. Jones arrived, he came quietly but with three other policemen, all looking serious and grim. Sgt. Jones showed Lon the search warrant and Lon proceeded to take the Sgt up to the third floor and showed Sgt. Jones the bag near the bed where Tim Trotter slept. Sgt. Jones had one of the other police officers put on plastic gloves and picked up the bag. The gloved officer put his hand into the bag and pulled out a small vial of some kind of liquid that had a stopper that could dose out drops.

Sgt. Jones said it looked suspicious and he would take it back to the station and have it examined by their lab to determine what was in the vial. In the meantime, the Sgt told Lon not to say anything to anyone about what had just happened under penalty of being charged with impeding an investigation.

Lon agreed to say nothing and was told to try to act natural around the upstairs residents so they wouldn't suspect anything.

The police left quietly with Lon standing there dumbfounded.

Of course, Derek called to check on how things were going and Lon said he was sworn to secrecy but Derek deduced that something had been found and that the police were involved.

What would happen next?

It turned out that the next thing that would happen was the Sunday morning church service. All of the above had occurred on a Saturday afternoon so since the next day was Sunday, Beth and Derek arrived at church early to help with set up and for Beth to practice with the choir. Both Beth and Derek had trouble concentrating on the morning's events because they were wondering what the police had found and whether or not someone would be arrested for the Congressman's murder.

As the service began and others began coming into the sanctuary they were able to focus on the service and put the murder and it's aftermath out of their minds for now.

More people had begun attending services after the killing to see what the church was all about and some continued to come back, finding comfort and meaning in the liberal church's practices and principles. Nothing like drama to bring out the ghouls.

As Rev. Stewart began her message, people were listening closely to what she had to say. Rev. Stewart talked about forgiveness and justice needing to happen at the same time. Forgiveness for the killer who's motive was still unknown and justice for the Congressman so that his killing would not go unpunished but would show that the justice system worked in this country. A big order!. Many said "Amen" to the Rev's sentiments as she called for calm and careful deliberation.

As the last notes of the closing hymn were being sung, Beth sang along to Amazing Grace again and hoped that justice would prevail.

CHAPTER FIFTEEN

The next day saw more drama as several police cars pulled up at the front of the church house and officers piled out quickly and ran up the steps to the door. Lon was in the office and let the officers in. Sgt. Jones was leading them and told Lon that they had to be taken upstairs quietly and let in the third floor and that Lon should stay downstairs for his safety.

Lon gave Sgt. Jones the key to the third floor and waited downstairs as the police ran up the stairs and then there was no sound for a few minutes before Lon began hearing shouts and loud noises.

Suddenly several policemen were escorting Tim Trotter down the stairs in handcuffs.Tim was yelling that he hadn't done anything but the police kept on coming and led him out the front door to a waiting squad car, putting him in the back seat still in handcuffs.

All the time, Tim was screaming that he was innocent, that he hadn't done anything wrong.

Lon later recounted all this to Beth and Derek when they came by the church house after they had heard via the grapevine what had happened.

"I feel terrible." said Lon, "but what else could I do?"

Beth said, "You did what you had to do." I just hope that Tim is the killer, not someone else."

So Beth and Derek went to their respective jobs hoping justice had been served.

While at work, Derek learned that 50 million of the dollars that Congressman Smith had been going to announce at the dinner where he died was in fact coming to the city of Detroit as a grant to help improve neighborhood businesses which had been struggling for many years as Detroit lost more and more of its population to the suburbs. In order to qualify, businesses would have to present a plan to show how they would use the grant and how it would positively impact the area near the business. And Derek would be in charge of this effort. He was thrilled to have been chosen to lead this but also aware of all the political traps that would present themselves. This could make or break his career. But he would do his best!

When he got home and told Beth about being put in charge of this grant money, she hugged him and said she knew he could do it and do it well.

"So why don't we celebrate by going out to dinner?" suggested Beth.

"That would be fantastic." replied Derek.

They checked on Charity who was still recovering but doing much better and set off for one of their favorite restaurants in the area, the Traffic Jam, which was also near the church.

After reviewing the menu, they both decided on the Caesar Salad with chicken with an order of sweet potatoes fries to celebrate Derek's being given an important job that could result in a big promotion if things turned out well.

They enjoyed a pleasant meal and even ran into a few friends to wave "Hi" to.

As they left the restaurant in mid evening and walked across the street to the parking lot from T. J.'s, they were feeling full and in a good mood.

But suddenly, a man in a ski mask came up behind

them and put a gun to Derek's head, saying "Don't move or I'll blow your head off. Give me your wallet NOW."

Beth and Derek froze and Derek complied with the demand for his wallet. Luckily, he kept his ID in his pocket and didn't carry any credit cards with him so the thief got around $100 in cash. But as the man backed away from them, he said, "Tim didn't kill that guy. Someone else did."

"What was that all about?" Derek said quietly as his breath slowed down to a normal rate and Beth started gasping.

"I guess it means that maybe Tim Trotter is innocent, but who knows if that guy knew what he was talking about." replied Beth.

Beth queried "Should we call the police?"

"I guess so." replied Derek who took out his cell phone and punched in 911. When an operator answered and Derek told her what had happened, she said that she would send a scout car around as there was one in the area that was free.

Soon lights were flashing and a police car pulled into the parking lot where they were standing next to Derek's car.

The officer got out of his car and introduced himself as Officer Twining, a light complexioned Black man, who was friendly and asked for their ID. Both Beth and Derek got out their driver's licenses and showed them to the officer who took themto his car where he ran a quick check and then handed back the ID's.

Since it was getting a little chilly, Officer Twining invited them to sit in his patrol car while he took down their statements. Derek explained what happened but could not give a description of the thief as the man had on a ski mask and didn't let Derek turn around during the robbery and Beth had been so stunned, she was afraid to look. Derek was able to say that when he handed the man the money, the thief's hands appeared to be olive colored, suggesting a light skinned Black man or possibly a Hispanic or Arab.

Derek had not noticed any kind of speech accent so that didn't narrow it down but Officer Twining told them he would write up the report and that Derek should come in the following morning to sign his statement. Derek agreed and the police car drove off.

"I've never had that happen." Derek was flummoxed as was Beth who had spent their lives trying to help others and had never encountered any violence directed at them.

"Well, now we know how others might feel in these circumstances." But what did the guy mean about Tim being innocent?" opined Beth. "That makes no sense."

They went home feeling anxious and still bringing their heart rates down to a normal level.

At least Charity was feeling better and came to greet them when they walked in the house. She even meowed a little which was her way of greeting them.

Beth picked her up and cuddled her, beginning to feel better. They stumbled to their bedroom, changed into nightclothes and lay down with Charity between them, purring loudly.

After a somewhat fretful night involving intermittent sleep, they got up and proceeded to go to their respective jobs with the plan that Derek would stop at the police station and sign his statement.

In the cold light of dawn, the previous night seemed bizarre but they tried to put it out of their heads for now, agreeing to discuss it again later that day.

Beth had a full schedule of clients so tried to focus on them rather than herself. She did tell Karen Gardner, her fellow therapist, who gasped and then gave Beth a big hug.

"That's awful" said Karen.

"Yes, it was." replied Beth but luckily no one was hurt physically. " I'll have to practice some of the techniques I tell my clients to do when they feel traumatized, like slow, deep breathing and focusing on some pleasant place to be."

Unfortunately her first client was Bill Duncan, the angry young man, who felt that the world was against him and seemed to be unable to find anything positive in his life.

But Beth let him talk and asked him to list his best attributes. At first he couldn't say he had any, but when she mentioned that he was young and in relatively good health, he actually smiled a little. She also mentioned that many would call him good looking (he was lean, tall and had a chiseled jaw). He seemed surprised to hear that but again smiled a little. He did say that since he was coming to counseling, his boss was being a little friendlier although he admitted that he still often felt angry at everybody.

Beth asked him if he would learn a breathing technique and he agreed to try it. So she asked him to sit comfortably, close his eyes and imagine himself in a pleasant place that was quiet and safe. Then she asked him to breathe in on the odd numbers and slowly breathe out on the even numbers, counting slowly to ten and also breathing in and out slowly herself. Then she asked him to tense up the muscles in his toes and then relax them. She continued asking him to tense muscles going up his legs, his abdomen, his hands, his forearms and his upper arms. The next step was shrugging his shoulders slowly and tilting his head, front, back, right and left but slowly. Finally, she asked him to lift his eyebrows, keeping his eyes closed then relax them. She then asked him to continue to breathe in and out slowly and encouraged him to let himself feel safe. He frowned at times but kept breathing slowly. And the last step, she counted backward from 10 to 1, breathing in on the even numbers and out on the odd ones. He did so and then Beth told him to slowly open his eyes.

He blinked and looked around. When she asked him how he felt, he answered he actually felt a little better.

"That's progress." said Beth.

Meanwhile, at the Wayne County Jail where Tim Trotter was being held in isolation, things weren't going well. Tim kept crying and shouting that he was innocent. He was having flashbacks to when he was at home and being locked in a closet by his alcoholic parents for some alleged transgression at the age of four. It went down hill from there. His parents took out their frustrations on him and he was unable to defend himself. They explained bruises to others by saying he was so clumsy that he kept falling down. More like I was pushed, thought Tim.

Where school could have been a refuge for him, it

wasn't. He was small for his age (probably due to poor nutrition, among other reasons), so was bullied by the bigger boys usually when the teachers weren't looking. He found he could trust no one to help him so he sulked and planned revenge in his mind that he couldn't carry out. He didn't even have a pet for comfort and didn't want one as he knew his parents would somehow harm the pet.

Tim did poorly in school and realized that he needed to get out of high school and figure out a way to leave home and his abusive parents. His time finally came and he barely graduated from high school but was accepted into the U. S. Army. Unfortunately, his terrible childhood resulted in him not being able to follow orders and accept authority so he was asked to leave within months of his enlistment but at least wasn't given a dishonorable discharge.

Tim had been "raised" in Flint, Mi., a city that was reeling from plant closures and a fleeing population, so Tim set out for New York City, a place he had only heard about but was told that it was a crossroads of the world.

"Maybe I can make a new life there?" thought Tim.

Alas, it wasn't to be.

CHAPTER SIXTEEN

Derek was at work diligently looking at all the paperwork associated with his new assignment, ie: government contracts, union rules, city ordinances and more.

"How am I going to make this thing work? It's so complicated." thought Derek, but he knew that he had make it work and make it work well. The city didn't need any more projects that didn't pan out or boondoggles that got a few people rich but didn't help the city at large.

So Derek pored over all the material even though his head was swimming with details. Plus he still felt some anxiety over the recent robbery so he decided to call the police and ask if they had any leads on the case. He went through several people before he was put through to a clerk in the local precinct who at least was friendly and tried to answer his questions.

"No, there have been no new developments on your case. I'm sorry." said Ms.Penny.

Then Derek decided to try another tack. "Is there any way I can visit Tim Trotter?" asked Derek.

Ms. Penny said he would have to contact the jail and see what the rules were and who was allowed to see him. She did agree to transfer his call to the jail where the person who answered wasn't as friendly.

"Who are your and why do you want to visit this prisoner?" said the disembodied voice on the phone.

"Wow?" thought Derek, but he proceeded to explain that he was a member of the First UU Church and had met Tim who had been working at the church.

Derek said he just wanted to see if Tim was all right and if there was anything he could do.

"Well," said the voice," you'll have to talk to his court appointed attorney and get clearance to visit him."

So Derek got the name and phone number of the attorney and called his office. It was Attorney Jacob Ford who actually answered the phone and spent some time talking with Derek to ascertain his reasons for visiting. Jacob said that Tim had no known family and was feeling pretty lonely and also insisted that he was innocent, so maybe a visit from a church member would be helpful. Jacob explained the visiting procedures at the Wayne County Jail and the times for visiting. He said that he would contact the jail and have Derek put on the approved visitor's list.

It turned out that Derek could actually visit now so he decided to do that and try to clear his head from all the work stuff that was making him feel that he was drowning in paper work.

Derek drove to the jail and found a nearby parking place, paid the parking fee and walked across the street to the jail.

Derek went into the jail facility and signed in to see Tim Trotter. He had to go through a stiff security process, was wanded and patted down. He had to show identification which was copied and then told to sit down and wait.

"Well, that went well." muttered Derek.

After sitting for about fifteen minutes he was called to the front desk and escorted by an armed guard through a door and down a hall that was silent as a tomb, although there were probably many people in this building.

"Good sound proofing," thought Derek.

He was taken to a door where the guard opened the door and told Derek to enter. He did so and found a small room with a glass partition in the middle of the room. There was one chair and a counter in front of the glass. On the other side of the glass, was it's identical counterpart. The guard escorted Derek to the chair and said the prisoner would enter through the door on the other side of the partition. Fairly soon, Tim Trotter, in orange jail uniform, with his hands handcuffed in front of him and his feet shackled shuffled into the room followed by another armed guard.

Tim was told to sit down in the chair which he did. Tim looked tired, thin and in poor spirits. He looked up to see Derek on the other side of the partition and did a double take.

"What are you doing here?" said Tim.

"That's a good question." replied Derek. "Believe it or not, I'm here to see how you are doing and if you need anything."

"What I need is a good lawyer because I didn't do anything wrong and I didn't kill the Congressman. I always get blamed for things and my life is one big hell!"

Derek looked closely at Tim and actually believed him. Derek didn't see Tim as having the moxie to pull off such a crime, let alone a reason to do so.

"We only have a few minutes to talk, so tell me everything that happened, so I can try to figure out what's going on." offered Derek.

As Tim told his story, Derek listened quietly and pondered what he could do?

Tim said supposedly someone had found some kind of substance in a bag near his bed and this substance was some kind of peanut oil that could have caused the Congressman's death. Tim said he didn't even know what anaphalayctic shock was, had never heard of it even.

Derek was only allowed to see Tim for 20 minutes so said that he would try to check into things and would visit Tim again soon.

The guard escorted Derek out of the visiting area and gave him back his ID and other items that had been confiscated when he was put through security. Derek walked out of the jail, wondering what he could do, what did it all mean and who killed the Congressman, if Tim didn't do it?

CHAPTER SEVENTEEN

On the other side of town, Beth was at the Wayne County Airport, getting ready to go to Rochester, New York, to go to her high school reunion. She had thought about not going but she already had her ticket, which wasn't cheap and felt an obligation to her old friends from her hometown of Milton, New York.

She knew Derek would take care of Charity and she would be back in a few days, so reluctantly boarded the plane and settled herself down for the hour trip to Rochester.

She hoped she'd have a good time but knew that she didn't have a lot in common with her old friends, some of whom she had known since kindergarten. She also wondered if her old high school boyfriend would be there but again. She hadn't talked to him in years and no longer had anything in common, but getting away for a few days might be refreshing and help her stop thinking about her clients and how to help them. She often felt a bond with her clients, most of whom were pretty likable. Some were not but she tried to help them anyway.

The time on the airplane "flew" by and she arrived at the Rochester Monroe County Airport in what seemed like no time. She had arranged for a rental car so she could get around the area on her own and hopefully visit a few people from the old days.

She had some cousins in the area and had let some of them know she would be in town so a small family reunion had been planned that evening at the home of her cousin, Bill. Beth had booked a room at a Best Western near the airport, so got her one suitcase from baggage claim and went to the car rental desk. She had a short wait, got her car and then realized that she needed to figure out how to drive it. Her own car was very old and she didn't drive it that often. The newer cars had so many more bells and whistles that it took her awhile to find the way to turn on the headlights. She didn't even bother to try to turn on the radio for the short drive to the hotel.

As she drove out of the airport parking lot, she wondered what was happening in Detroit and if Tim Trotter had been the one to kill Congressman Smith.

"Oh well," she thought, "focus on the hear and now and try to enjoy her small vacation."

After checking into her hotel, she called her longtime friend she had known since kindergarten, Sandy Fowler. Beth knew the phone number by heart as Sandy had had the same landline phone number for over 40 years. Sandy answered right away as she had been expecting the call.

"How are you? " asked Sandy.

"Tired but here at the hotel." They chatted for quite awhile as Sandy was a "talker".

The reunion was the next evening at a restaurant outside of Milton but wasn't until 6 pm, so Beth agreed to meet Sandy in Milton for lunch as the only restaurant in town called the Arlington, named after a long defunct hotel that had once stood by the railroad tracks, Milton's previous claim to fame as the train used to go through twice a day on the way to Buffalo, New York. The hotel had been torn down years ago but a small restaurant had been built on a corner of the downtown area and did serve alcohol, so it was also the town's only bar. They agreed to meet at 12 noon but Beth arrived a little early after getting a good night's sleep.

She had talked to Derek in the early evening who told her about his visiting Tim and wondering if Tim had actually killed the Congressman. Derek said he would check out some leads and Beth pleaded with him to be careful. Derek promised he would and said that Charity was doing much better now. She was actually walking around the house meowing and looking for Beth, so Beth talked into the phone so Charity could hear her. This seemed to calm Charity down a little.

Walking into the Arlington, Beth felt a little strange as she didn't recognize anyone. A bunch of guys were sitting at the bar and drinking bottled beer. One person looked a little familiar but she wasn't sure who it was.

Soon Sandy came into the restaurant and they were led to a table in a corner. Sandy and Beth hugged and sat down to order. Beth had always gotten root beer floats when she was a child at a soda fountain so ordered one for old time sake. Of course, a cheeseburger and fries were de rigeur too.

Beth and Sandy stayed and talked for a long time after finishing their lunches but both decided they needed to go back and take a nap to get ready for the reunion. Beth had come back to see old friends but since she hadn't lived in Milton for many years, she always knew she had little in common with many of her former classmates. So she felt both happy and anxious to be at her high school reunion. She never talked about politics as she knew many of the people she grew up with were dyed in the woolconservative politically and most had never lived in a large city and had had little contact with people different from themselves. They seldom said outright racist comments but sometimes did make statements about "those people" meaning some minority group as a generalization about how "those people" didn't work hard enough or took advantage of government benefits. Beth had learned that it was difficult to discuss their ideas in any detail and many of her old school friends were careful what they said around her.

But they could talk about old times and the silly things they did which would now be considered mild but at the time was seen as very shocking, ie: like drinking beer and smoking cigarettes while being underage. They had heard very little about marijuana or other harder drugs at the time. The current climate of drug overdoses and drug cartels that reportedly existed in other countries could not have been imagined when they were in high school. So talk about stealing laundry from someone's clothes line or silly pranks for Halloween still made them smile.

Beth ate some good food and drank a little but knowing that she had to drive herself back to the hotel, she stopped after one drink. She did catch up with several former classmates and learned what they were doing for work and were still raising children. Beth wondered what would have happened to her if she had stayed at home and gone to a local college. But she would never know as she choose to go to a distant school and had chosen to live in a large city and learn more about life and people different from herself.

So she said a fond farewell and got herself back to her hotel to get some sleep for her early morning flight back to Detroit and wondered what was happening back in her new home town of Detroit.

CHAPTER EIGHTEEN

It was barely light outside when a lone figure left the church house and walked to a nearby bus stop.

CHAPTER NINETEEN

Derek was missing Beth but still felt determined to do the best he could to help find the murderer. He had also been working hard on his work assignment and had made some progress by setting up a task force and giving them different areas to focus on: determining exactly what the parameters of the grant were, what the goals of the grant were as written in their proposal and asking for community input on how best to make the money have the biggest impact in the community. He and his task force had been working now for several weeks and he felt that he could take some time off from his job to go to the church house and talk with Lon Hardigan.

When he arrived at the church house, Lon was talking with Rod Harrison, a man whom Derek had spoken with earlier about Tim Trotter. Rod said "Hello" and then said he had to get back to work to finish cleaning the floor of the sanctuary.

Lon said he had no new information about the murder but was trying to keep an open mind.

But he did say that the police had been back to go over the "scene of the crime" and had also gone back upstairs to check out everything there. They were there for a few hours, then left without saying anything to anyone.

Derek and Lon talked for a while about how things were going at the church. Nothing like a murder to bring in the curious. There were more visitors on Sundays which they both thought was primarily for gawkers. But some of the visitors did keep coming back so in a strange way, the murder was good for business.

Lon did tell Derek that Tim Trotter had just shown up on the church house doorstep a few months ago and asked if he could work at the church. Since they had an extra bed upstairs, he decided to try him out and even though he wasn't the best worker, they decided to continue to work with him and see if they could improve his work performance so he would have more marketable skills and a good recommendation for his next job.

CHAPTER TWENTY

Beth was so glad to be back home after her reunion trip that she hugged Charity and hugged Derek even harder. But she had to go back to work and had a lot of clients that day as she had had to reschedule some to allow her to leave for her vacation.

The first schedule for the day was Julia Bunting, who as usual was tearful and saying no one liked her and complaining about how her family treated her. She tended to feel sorry for herself and was not able to look at her own behavior as to how that might have played and was still playing out in her relationships. She came from a large family and her father apparently had had a drinking problem. Money was tight they were basically working class in terms of class status. She never thought of going to college and had not done that well in school grade-wise.

She had started working part time in a small restaurant as a teen and fallen in love with the very married manager but began a love affair that lasted for several years. The "boyfriend" at some point ended the affair and Julia felt devastated so she moved to Florida where she ended up working in real estate and did well.

She did eventually marry an older man who was morbidly obese but the marriage ended in divorce after a few years so she came back to Michigan and began developing medical problems which resulted in her being put on Social Security Disability. She was living on a small monthly stipend and an older brother moved in with her to help them both financially. However, her brother was an alcoholic who did bring her to her appointments. She wanted to be seen frequently and presented as a very "needy" person.

Beth's goal with her was to help her recognize her strengths and begin to build on them to improve her self esteem and see herself in a more positive light but it was not easy going by a long shot.

So today, Beth let Julia moan and complain for awhile then redirected the conversation to what she wanted from life at this point---what were her short and long term goals?

Once the session was over, Beth was emotionally tired but let go of the frustration and moved on the next client.

CHAPTER TWENTY ONE

Derek decided to visit Tim Trotter at the jail and since he was on the visiting list, he could go anytime during visiting hours.

Tim looked even worse this time than he did the last time. His face was drawn, he had bags under his eyes and had a fearful look about him--"a deer in the headlights" look. Tim talked softly and still insisted he was innocent of killing the Congressman and said he hadn't even known the Congressman or anything about him. Why would he want to kill him?

They chatted for a few minutes and Derek told Tim that he had put some money in his jail account so Tim could buy a few things, like toothpaste, candy, whatever. Tim thanked Derek but left the interview looking very defeated.

In the meantime, Beth had decided to visit the slain Congressman's local office to give her condolences and to see how things were going there.

She had called ahead and was told she was welcome to visit anytime. She got her car and drove to the office that was located near downtown. It was just a small storefront that still had the Congressman's name on the door. Since his death, someone else would be appointed to take his place eventually but that could take a long time to sort out. His constituents would not have any representation for now.

Beth knocked and entered, realizing that boxes were being packed and the office was being dismantled, but a friendly young woman came forward and greeted Beth with smile.

"What can I do for you? She said.

Beth explained who she was and that she had been present when the Congressman had been poisoned. Beth said she was so sorry that it had happened and couldn't understand why someone would want to have killed him.

The young woman, whose name was Tamika Harris, accepted the sentiments offered and thanked Beth for coming. Tamika said that every political person or office holder had enemies and that death threats were not uncommon for many of them.

However, Tamika intimated that the Congressman "got around" and that some people might have been angry at him for his personal behavior, but still didn't make murder the way to handle a disagreement or get revenge.

Beth didn't think it would be appropriate to ask Tamika to explain what she was talking about but it did give her a possible lead to check out.

Rod Harrison finished up his assigned tasks at the church, then left to go to the library. Rod was a tall, thin Euro-American with a receding hairline but still wore his remaining hair long so that he resembled an aging "hippie." Rod had been living at the church for several years and had seemed to fit in well with the other left leaning types who preferred to do manual work while they took college courses or worked on other projects.

At the library, Rod settled in at a computer. He didn't have one of his own but wanted to check something out. He typed out pedophile, spelling it incorrectly several times before he got it right. Then he read what he could find about the topic, theories about what causes a person to sexually abuse children, often pedophiles were themselves sexually abused as children so while they don't like the behavior, they feel drawn to it later in life. He read about "grooming", how an adult gains the trust of a young person, often giving them gifts and lots of attention, often to those who were not getting good attention in their homes.

Rod thought about his own childhood and how his parents worked hard but never had time for he and his five siblings, just trying to get food on the table and keep a roof over their head. His mother was somewhat cold and his father had been raised by a gruff father who believed in physical punishment so Rod's father continued the family tradition, leaving Rod feeling unloved. Rod was struggling with the anger from his childhood at how he had been treated and still trying to find his way in the bigger world.

CHAPTER TWENTY TWO

Derek got a call from the jail to learn that Tim had been badly beaten by other prisoners and was being hospitalized with his injuries. They were severe but he was expected to recover eventually.

Derek rushed over to Detroit Receiving Hospital to find Tim in a room with a police guard standing outside the door. Since Derek had clearance to visit Tim at the jail, he was allowed to visit Tim at the hospital. Derek was frisked by the guard and had to hand over his cell phone and pens before he was allowed to enter Tim's room.

Tim looked terrible. He had bandages on both arms and around his head but he was awake. Derek said how sorry he was that he had been attacked and asked if there was anything he could do.

"You can clear my name." said Tim. "They set me up to be attacked, leaving me alone in the yard for awhile for the first time. Several guys came up and started hitting me and punching me before some guards came over to stop them. They were yelling that I was a killer."

"Oh, my God," replied Derek. "That's awful. I'll ask around and try to see if they can make sure you're guarded at all times at the jail. And I'll also keep trying to find out what happened to Congressman Smith. I'll come visit you again either in the hospital or at the jail. Take care and try not to worry."

Beth had a difficult day at work. The previous night she had received a call from one of her clients. (She always gave her home phone number so clients could call if they needed to.) It was a young male client, Kenneth Grant, whom she had been seeing for a few weeks. He was working in a factory but was a heroin addict, after getting started on pain pills. He had been abstinent for a few weeks but had gotten a hold of a lot of heroin the night before and while his girlfriend was out with her girlfriends, he had taken all the heroin. Because he had been abstinent for awhile, this caused an overdose and he technically "died." His girlfriend came home just after he had "died" She called EMS and they administered Narcan and he was brought back to life. He seemed a little proud of what he had done.

I talked him through what had happened and why he thought he had relapsed. He presented with a blunted affect which was usual for him and still seemed nonchalant about the whole episode.

He agreed to go to more 12 step meetings but because everyone in his family had died from one kind of overdose or another (both his parents died from alcoholism, his younger brother had died a few years earlier from heroin), he admitted that he thought that was the way he was supposed to die too.

Beth felt uncomfortable about the episode so talked to her supervisor to see if there was something more she could do. They agreed to refer him to the clinic psychiatrist for an evaluation for possible anti-depressant medication. However, Kenneth was reluctant to see a psychiatrist or take any psychiatric medication. It would take some persuasion to get him to change his mind.

What Beth didn't know was that the drug dealer who

had sold Kenneth the illegal heroin had heard about Kenneth's overdose and was worried that Kenneth might tell someone where he got the drug. So the drug dealer was quietly keeping an eye on Kenneth and knew that he went to some mental health clinic for therapy. This drug dealer wanted to find out who Kenneth's therapist was and make sure that no one revealed to the police his connection to the overdose.

So unbeknownst to Beth, Kenneth had a car following him when he went to the clinic and that car waited outside while Kenneth was inside the clinic. The driver took note of the clinic's information and gave it to the drug dealer sometime later that day.

Derek felt more certain than ever that Tim did not kill the Congressman but had no idea of how to prove it other than finding out who the real killer was. When Beth told him about her visit to the deceased Congressman's office and that a staffer had said that the Congressman had a negative reputation to some, Derek wondered what that meant and if this was somehow part of the puzzle?

So Derek went online to look up the Congressman and if there were any stories about things the Congressman had done that were suspicions.

An article in a Washington, D. C. paper from over 15 years ago mentioned that a lawsuit had been filed against the Congressman for inappropriate behavior but didn't say what the behavior was. It did say that a settlement had been reached and that all parties were under court order not to discuss the settlement.

"Hmm?" thought Derek. "That's certainly weird."

So Derek went online to the files for that newspaper to

try to learn more if he could.

CHAPTER TWENTY TWO

The following Sunday the service at the church was focused on the topic of "Good Overcoming Evil" and Rev. Stewart talked passionately about the importance of not responding to bad actions with more bad actions.

The music reinforced this theme as usual and Beth had tears in her eyes when they all sang the old hymn "Amazing Grace", written by John Newton, a former slave ship captain who later in life found redemption and wrote a hymn that is now sung all over the world, a hymn about "I once was lost, but now am found, was blind but now I see."

At coffee hour after the service, Beth found it difficult to look at the area where the Congressman has been poisoned and later died.

"What an awful thing to happen in a place where violence is shunned. Why, why, why." thought Beth.

Derek had stayed home from church while he continued to check the internet for sources regarding Congressman Smith's legal settlements. Surprisingly he found one article that mentioned a settlement with a young man. "That's strange." thought Derek. "Why a young man? I thought he may have sexually harassed a young woman?"

The date on the settlement was 10 years earlier—1996. Derek kept reviewing as many websites as he could to see if there were other legal disputes or settlements that involved the Congressman. He couldn't find any.

In order to better understand Tim, Derek decided that he needed to go to New York City and talk to the people who had known Tim before he came to Detroit. He had some time coming from work, so called Beth and left a message as to what he planned to do, then called and got a ticket to New York, went home and packed and drove himself to the airport for a plane that was leaving in two hours.

As Derek was boarding his plane, he was thinking, "Maybe I acted a little hastily, but I'm on my way so let's see what I can find in New York."

Derek had gotten the address of the storefront in NYC from Beth's friend, Fatima, so caught a cab and went straight to that address.

He, too, found a dingy looking place but there were some people milling around in front, so Derek went in, carry on bag et al. He asked to speak to a manager or supervisor, so was taken into an office at the back of the building.

A man whose hygiene looked compromised said "Hello, how can I help you?"

Derek explained that he was a friend of Tim Trotter's and that Tim was now in jail for allegedly killing Congressman Smith a few weeks earlier. The man, whose name was Rashid Brown asked Derek for identification which he gave.

Then Rashid said he hadn't known Tim well and that he had only been at the center for a few short months before he took off and they didn't know exactly where he was going and why, but that Tim seemed a "lost soul".

"He didn't seem like a bad guy, just someone who didn't know who he was or what he was doing," said Rashid.

Rashid hadn't noticed any sense of violence about Tim

but he also hadn't worked with him closely.

Derek asked if anyone knew Tim better and Rashid said that he didn't think so but would ask around. He took Derek's contact information and said he would get back to Derek if he found out anything further.

Derek thanked him and walked out the door, standing on the curb, getting ready to cross the street.

Derek had never been in New York City before and didn't realize how crazy New York drivers could be, so he stepped off the curb thinking it was safe to cross the street when "WHAM", Derek was plowed into by a cab with the cab driver shouting something in a foreign language at Derek as he drove into him.

Derek went down in the street like a sack of potatoes and hit his head on the pavement. Several people screamed and the cab driver did stop and called 911 for help on his radio. Derek felt his world go black and then he didn't remember anything until he woke up in a hospital bed with tubes sticking out of him and being strapped down so he couldn't move. His head was bandaged and he felt like crap but at least he was alive! It seemed like forever but eventually someone came in his room—a short dark skinned woman who said she was his nurse, Serena. Serena asked him how he was feeling and Derek was able to respond with a "Not so well, but I'll live, I guess!"

"Well, at least, you're a feisty one." replied Serena.

"Where am I?, asked Derek.

"You're in New York Presbyterian Hospital in intensive care but it looks like you'll make it!"

Beth had been listed as his next of kin on some papers in his wallet so the hospital social worker called her several hours later and told Beth what had happened.

"Oh, my God, no!" cried Beth, but then she calmed herself down and asked for more information and asked to have the message relayed that she loved him and that she would fly to see him as soon as she could get a flight to LaGuardia Airport.

With her hands shaking, Beth dialed several friends and told them what had happened. One agreed to take her to the airport and another agreed to come and visit Charity at least once a day to feed and provide some company.

Beth contacted United Airlines and was able to get a flight that evening, so she hurriedly packed a small bag and was soon driven to the Detroit Metropolitan Airport to catch her flight.

All through the flight, Beth kept telling herself to slow her breathing down and take the same advice that she gave to clients. By the time she reached the New York Airport, she felt calmer.

Beth had arranged to stay with her friend, Fatima, who lived in Brooklyn, so took a cab to Fatima's apartment where she stayed for the night. She was able to get a message to Derek via hospital staff that she was in New York and would visit him in the morning.

"What the hell happened?" said Beth when she first saw Derek the following morning.

"It's a long story, but I'll survive." replied Derek.

Beth rushed up and hugged Derek, then sat down next to him so he could tell the story of how he stepped off a curb and was hit by cab. He said he had a broken wrist, lots of bruises, including a possible concussion, but that the doctor told him he should heal in time and only had to stay in the hospital for a few more days before he could be discharged back home. Derek said they want to keep observing me for awhile to make sure my brain isn't fried.

Beth gave a sigh of relief and said she would notify his job about what happened so that he could switch to sick time of which he had a lot, since he never got sick!

They talked for awhile and Derek told her what little he had learned from visiting the storefront where Tim Trotter had been involved but he didn't think this was a good lead. But he also told Beth about the information that he had learned from checking the newspaper morgue, ie: there had been a settlement between the Congressman and someone years ago but that no details were available that he could find but he planned to continue checking when he got back to Detroit and was stuck at home for several weeks while his arm and bruises healed.

Sure enough, several days later, Beth took Derek home in a rental car as it seemed it would be more comfortable for him and cheaper. It was a long drive from NYC, but they made it in one day.

Derek got settled in their home and Charity was so happy to see him that she jumped up in his lap, something she usually didn't do.

"Meow" said Charity. "Meow,

"Back at ya." said Derek.

Derek did call the jail and asked staff to let Tim Trotter know that he was convalescing at home after an accident and the he would visit Tim as soon as he was able. Since Beth had had to cancel all her clinic appointments for the time she went to NYC, she knew she had to go back into work and see how her clients were doing.

Her first client the day she got back was Bill Duncan who came in seething as usual.

"Why did you cancel my appointment?" fumed Bill.

"I'm really sorry but my boyfriend was in a bad accident in another city and was hospitalized so I needed to be there and make sure he was getting the care he needed. He's home now and doing better, but tell me how you've been doing since we last talked."

"Well, I feel like hell and the world is no better place than it was when I last saw you. In fact, maybe it's worse!"

"How so?" replied Beth.

"Remember I talked about a girlfriend before. Well, she dumped me. I was nice to her and gave her presents and everything."

"What did she say as to why she was breaking up with you? Asked Beth.

"She said I was always angry and she felt she couldn't trust me."

"Why do you think she said that? Is that true? asked Beth.

"I don't know. I know I'm angry a lot but I have reason to be. I have been treated bad for a long time," said Bill."I have a reason to be angry," Bill in a louder tone of voice.

"I'm sorry that you had such a tough time in your earlier life. Unfortunately, there is no way to change what has happened to you or to anyone." replied Beth.

"But do you think that hanging on to that anger is good for you? Does it alienate you from those who might like you. Is there anyway to refocus your anger. I'm not saying you aren't still angry but can you see that it's preventing you from being happier now? What would your life look like if you could control and re channel that anger?"

Bill looked confused. "I never thought of it that way before. You mean my anger is keeping me from feeling better, being happier?"

"Well, that might be a possibility" replied Beth. "What do you think that your life might look like if you didn't feel angry, even if you have a justification for being angry?"

"I have no idea," said Bill. "I can't remember not feeling angry."

"So your assignment for this coming week is to list all the things you would like to do that could make you feel better, whatever it is, no matter how big or how small. Then bring that list with you next week and we'll talk about each item on it to see why you think it would make you feel better, okay?" Beth finished.

"In fact, if you want to try one or two of them during the week, go ahead, but keep it small and don't let yourself feel bad if it doesn't work out right away."

Bill said, "I'll see what I can do, see you next week."

Derek was starting to feel better now that he was home and could relax. But he felt restless, so got on his computer and continued to try to scout out information about the Congressman's lawsuit which appeared to have happened about thirteen years ago. What could the Congressman have done that would result in him settling a lawsuit for an undisclosed sum?

Derek kept checking every source he could think of

but nothing was showing any new information.

CHAPTER TWENTY FOUR

The young man had checked what he could at the public library and didn't find what he was looking for, so he wondered if he was in the clear. Could someone who knew computers and online data a lot better than he did find out what had happened to him so many years ago? Maybe he'd have to take matters into his own hands.

So he slowly made his way back to his home and sat down, staring into space. What could he do to make sure he was safe? "Maybe I need to get a gun", he thought.

"No, no, that's too extreme, isn't it? What about a knife that could stop someone silently?"

Beth saw her next client, Stan Olds, whom she had been seeing for many years now, at his request. He was a retired welder from one of the auto plants who had a secure retirement income. He had been a functioning alcoholic but had finally stopped drinking when he was seeing a previous therapist. That therapist had transferred the case to Beth because she thought he might benefit from seeing a different person.

Stan was initially wary of a new therapist and thought he had been "let go" by his former counselor. He was feeling abandoned but did come to see Beth twice a month at first and he seemed to feel comfortable with Beth. Beth had grown to like Stan and continued to reinforce abstinence and help him sort out that damage he had done to his family during all his years of daily drinking.

Stan also saw his physician regularly and had signed a

release so that Beth could talk to his doctor. Stan was a former marine who took pride in his past military service and had been honorably discharged. Stan often wore a cap that had the Marine insignia on it, was always on time and invariably polite.

Today, Stan talked about his ex-wife and his children, all of whom he had helped financially as he was in a position to do so. He continued to help them at times with major purchases and from his remarks, they didn't seem to be taking advantage of him.

Stan presented with a somewhat flat affect most of the time, but his underlying anxiety was right below the surface. His mother had died when he was twelve years old and his father had sent he and his slightly younger brother to a boarding school in Mexico. Stan's dad was of Mexican heritage while his mother had been of Irish descent. Stan had felt abandoned and alienated from his father when he was sent away and never really recovered from this trauma. They went back to live with their father after two years at the school but the damage had been done.

Beth found that if she just listened and offered support, this was the best she could do for Stan. Stan tended to be hyperverbal and could talk without interruption for a long time. Today, Stan talked and talked and Beth reminded him of all the good things he had done and all the people he had helped which he needed to hear.

Stan asked Beth if he could call her if he needed to and she replied in the affirmative as she always did, but he rarely called. He just needed to know that he could.

When Beth got in her car to leave the clinic, she

noticed an older model car sitting at the back of the lot with a long male figure in the driver's seat.

"Well, maybe it's nothing." thought Beth as she began to drive away. But just then, the older car fired up and started following her. "What is going on?" She didn't recognize the driver or the car. The driver had a ball cap on his head pulled down so you couldn't see his face.

So Beth sped up taking the fastest route to her house. The mysterious car kept following her.

As Beth pulled up in her driveway, the other car drove past her house and didn't stop.

"Whew! Maybe I'm paranoid." said Beth to herself.

She waited a few minutes before getting out of the car and hurried into the house to be greeted by Derek and Charity.

Derek was slowly recovering from his trauma, his arm was still in a cast but his bumps and bruises had gone through the color stages from purple to blue to yellow. He felt like he could move better and wasn't as sore. Charity kept an eye on him at all times and usually sat next to him while he was watching television or working on his computer.

He felt thankful to be alive and realizes how close he had come to being killed on that street in New York.

"I don't care if I never go back to New York City. Detroit is way safer than that place." grumbled Derek

Beth had gotten word to Tim Trotter in the jail that Derek had been injured while away and that he couldn't visit, but that he was still trying to find out who really killed the Congressman.

She had gone to the clinic to see clients while Lon Hardigan had stopped by to see how Derek was doing.

Lon and Derek chatted for some time, with Lon telling Derek that he still didn't understand what had happened and wondered if they'd ever find out the truth.

Lon hasn't come by car to visit Derek so it appeared that no one but Derek was home that morning. Beth had gone to work and Derek was lounging in the living room with Charity when Lon first came.

At some point Lon asked if he could "use the facilities" and was of course, granted permission. So Lon walked upstairs to the bathroom.

It was at that point that a man came running from the kitchen with a knife and tried to stab Derek. Derek was so taken aback that at first he didn't realize what was happening but soon his survival instincts took over and and he fought back, hitting the assailant with his cast with deflected the knife for a time.

Hearing the commotion, Lon came running down the stairs just as Charity was preparing to bite the intruder, but Lon got there first and hit the man in the head with a candlestick that was on the mantle.

Both Lon and Derek were stunned to recognize the intruder as Rod Harrison, one of the occupants of the Church House who helped with care taking at the church.

Rod was knocked out by the blow to his head but Lon quickly called 911 and asked for a police car as there had been an attempted murder, giving the address.

Surprisingly, the police arrived in 15 minutes while Rod was beginning to wake up.

"Why did you try to kill Derek?" said a stunned Lon.

"I thought he'd find out that I was part of a legal settlement many years ago when that miserable

Congressman settled out of court rather than be found guilty of sexual abuse of a minor. He deserved to die and I'm not sorry I did it." replied Rod.

Derek answered with "Oh my God. I didn't know that. I couldn't find out who or what the settlement was about."

As the police hauled Rod away, Derek and Lon sat there stunned and luckily neither had been seriously hurt by the attack.

EPILOGUE

Beth and Derek settled in for a quiet night of tv watching with Tim Trotter over as a guest for dinner. Beth had made her famous turkey meatloaf that had gone over well with Tim who was so glad to get out of jail that Spam would have tasted good.

"I can't believe that my own roommate would kill someone and frame me for murder," said Tim, "but I'm glad that this nightmare is over. Despite everything I like Detroit and want to stay here and try to make a life for myself."

"Welcome to the "D" and we'll help in any way that we can." replied Beth.

Charity was sleeping peacefully on the couch and planned to remain there for the rest of the evening.

Sally N. Borden is a retired psychiatric social worker who worked in her field for 54 years. She has been a member of the First

Unitarian-Universalist Church of Detroit since 1973.

Made in the USA
Monee, IL
07 November 2020